This book belongs to

....

....

....

....

This is a Bright Sparks Book.
First published 2000
Bright Sparks
Queen Street House,
4, Queen Street,
Bath, BA1 1HE, UK.
Copyright © Parragon 2000

Produced for Parragon Books by
Oyster Books Ltd, Unit 4, Kirklea Farm,
Badgworth, Somerset, BS26 2QH, UK

Illustrated by Andrew Geeson
Written by Marilyn Tolhurst

Printed in Italy

ISBN 1 84250 064 3

BIRTHDAY BEAR

Illustrated by Andrew Geeson

Bright ☆ Sparks

Rosie woke up, jumped out of bed, and ran into Danny's room. "Guess what day it is!" she shouted.

"It's Saturday," muttered Danny, grumpily. "And it's raining, too."

"I know it's Saturday, silly," exclaimed an excited Rosie. "But it's my birthday!"

Rosie spotted Jack the letter carrier coming up the path. She ran downstairs to meet him.

"There's nothing for you," he teased.

But Jack's bag was bulging!

"You can open your cards when Dad comes in," laughed Mom. "But the birthday girl needs her breakfast first."

Rosie could hardly wait.

After breakfast, they all watched while Rosie opened a big pile of cards and presents.

"I got a card from Conker," said Rosie, giving him a big kiss. "It's got his pawprint on!"

They spent the morning getting the house ready for Rosie's birthday party. They blew up balloons and hung up streamers until everything looked perfect.

"That looks lovely," announced Mom, finally. "I can see Joe down by the pond. Why don't you go and feed the ducks while I finish everything else?"

Danny and Rosie ran through the orchard and waved to Joe the farm worker. It had stopped raining, but it was still very wet and muddy.

"Happy birthday, Rosie," called Joe.

When they reached the pond, Rosie noticed something floating at the edge of the water, all tangled up in the weeds.

"Look over there, Danny," cried Rosie. "What is that muddy blob floating in the water?"

"I'll go in and see," said Danny, splashing into the pond
and wading out toward the strange object. He took three steps,
then stopped.

"Go on," called Rosie. "What's the matter?"

Danny began to giggle.

"I can't move," he said. "My boots are stuck in the mud!"

Rosie started to laugh, too. Danny wriggled, pulled, twisted, and turned, trying to free his boots from the mud.

Suddenly, Danny's foot slipped out of his boot and he fell bottom-first into the water with a huge splash.

Joe came across to see what all the laughter was about. He held out his hand to Danny.

"What's that muddy mess you're holding?" he chuckled.

"I don't know," replied a very wet and muddy Danny, pulling weeds out of his hair. "Here–you can have it, Rosie."

"It's a bear!" cried Rosie, taking the soggy bundle into her arms. "A poor muddy old bear."

"I wonder how he got there," said Danny.

Dripping wet and covered with mud, Danny and Rosie walked back to the house.

"What have you been up to?" laughed Mom. "And what on earth have you got there?"

Mom took the bear from Rosie.

"Oh dear! I think all three of you need a bath before the party starts."

In no time at all, Rosie, Danny, and the little bear were clean and ready for the party.

"Wow! Come and see the cake, Rosie," said Danny. "It looks terrific!"

Rosie tied a big yellow bow around the bear's neck and sat him on the window sill to watch the party.

At bedtime, Rosie sighed, "That was the best birthday party ever. I love being five. Do you know what my best present was, Mommy?" she asked.

"What was that?" asked Mom.

"My little bear. I wish I could keep him."

"Well, we'll have to wait and see" said Mom. "He might belong to someone."

The next day, Rosie made a "Lost Bear" poster, and Jack put it in the grocery window. A few weeks went by and nobody claimed the bear, so Rosie was allowed to keep him.

Rosie made up lots of stories about how the bear got into the pond. But they never did find out how he *really* got there.

"It doesn't matter where you came from," she told him. "You can live with us now. Billy Rabbit can be your best friend."

"What will you call him?" asked Danny.

"Birthday Bear, of course!" smiled Rosie.